I Have BEES in My brain

A Child's View of Inattentiveness

by TRISH HAMMOND

Illustrations by Chuck McIntosh

◆ FriesenPress

Suite 300 - 990 Fort St
Victoria, BC, V8V 3K2
Canada

www.friesenpress.com

ISBN
978-1-5255-1034-2 (Paperback)
978-1-5255-1035-9 (eBook)

1. JUVENILE FICTION

Distributed to the trade by The Ingram Book Company

Dedicated to those of you who picked up this book, and have already forgotten why.

Two of Queenie's playful bees were practicing their waggle dance inside Jasper's head, when suddenly their world turned sideways and they fell into each other.

"Ouch!" cried Brady. "I think you've bent one of my wings!"

"Don't worry," said Benkin. "You've got three others. Besides, it wasn't my fault." He glanced down at the restless boy who was slouched over his classroom desk. "I think Jasper woke up from his daydream."

daydream

Jasper was moving his head in circles. He had trouble sitting
still. Or standing in one spot. Or listening to a long
conversation. Today's lesson was **way** too long, so he let
his mind wander for the tenth time that morning.

He watched the girl beside him wrap a strand of hair around
her nose and then tuck the ends between her teeth. He
focused on the missing piece of tile on the floor, and then
thought about how uncomfortable these hard seats were.
He studied the big juice stain on the front of his shirt. Funny
how it made a shape like a dragonfly. If he traced the outline
with his fingers like so—

"Jasper?" a voice said.

Startled, Jasper knocked his books over. The teacher had asked him a question, but he had no idea what it was. He hated it when that happened. No wonder he couldn't follow any instructions. He had a sudden urge to nibble on the ends of his fingers.

Brady and Benkin bent their antennas in alarm. "Uh oh. The poor kid doesn't know what's going on. We'd better help out."

The bees stroked the hair on their chins, trying to think up helpful thoughts to fill Jasper's mind. Being careful not to overwhelm him, they gently let some suggestions fall into place, one by one.

nibble

I hate cereal for breakfast. PLUNK!

I wonder where my blue running shoes are. PLUNK!

Did my mom go to work today? PLUNK!

I think I need a haircut. PLUNK!

"Jasper," the teacher said again, "can you answer the question?"

"I'm hungry!" blurted out Jasper.

The teacher was about to explain that his hunger had nothing to do with what she'd just asked, when Jasper grabbed his knapsack and left the classroom.

Brady and Benkin looked at each other. "Too much?" asked Brady.

"Maybe just a little," replied Benkin.

Jasper sat outside the classroom door, with the bees quietly watching him. He'd had a lot more trouble concentrating lately; his head was always buzzing with random thoughts. He'd barely finished thinking about one thing, when something else popped into his head. That made it hard to get anything done.

He also hadn't been sleeping well. He knew that staying up late playing video games kept his brain awake and interfered with his sleep, but he couldn't break the habit.

The tag inside his t-shirt was rubbing against his neck, and just like that, he felt like he couldn't take it anymore. Not having the words he needed to express his frustration, he stood up and kicked the wall.

REGULATED

The bees were unsettled. With their front legs crossed behind their abdomens, they paced back and forth as they tried to figure out what was wrong with Jasper.

"I was just thinking," Brady began, "Queenie's been napping. Do you think that might have something to do with Jasper having more trouble concentrating?"

"You know, little bee," Benkin said, as he playfully tugged on Brady's stinger, "you might be on to something."

Brady puffed out his thorax and beamed. "When Queenie's awake, she helps to keep us **regulated**."

"That's a mighty big word for a little bee," Benkin started. "How about helping me out by explaining what that means?"

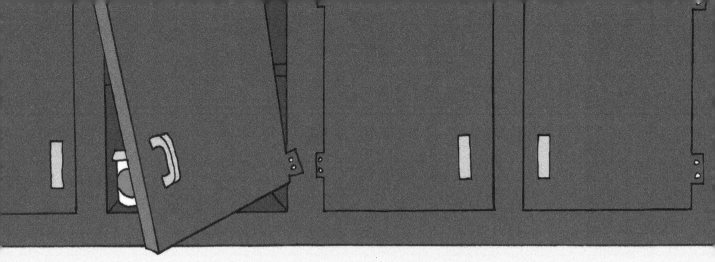

Brady needed no more encouragement. "Queenie acts like the brain's filter. When she's alert, she controls all the stuff we put in Jasper's head, making sure that we only tell him what he needs to know. Without her, we're buzzing this way and that way, and I think we might be confusing him a little."

"Uh huh," Benkin said. "Continue."

"Well, it's like what happened in the classroom. We put random thoughts in Jasper's head, and none of them connected to anything. Poor guy didn't know what idea he should be listening to. If Queenie was awake and doing her job, she'd tell us that we can't plant thoughts in his head like **cereal, shoes, mom, haircut,** and **hungry**, all at the same time."

"We can, if it's a hungry mom with a new haircut eating cereal from her shoes," Benkin chuckled.

"Aw, quit pulling my wings," Brady replied. "I'm trying to be serious here. We need some good strategies to help Jasper out."

Jasper was now wandering around the hallways, jumping up to hit every third ceiling tile. After falling down twice, he decided to swat the locker doors with his knapsack instead. The hallway lights were bright and bothering his eyes. And he still had no idea what the teacher had asked him.

Jasper hated feeling restless and fidgety all the time. He would have found it encouraging to know that it wasn't always his fault. Without a working regulator in his brain, it was hard for him to sort out his thoughts and to pay attention. He would like nothing more than to have the bees keep his ideas properly organized.

Benkin turned and stared into Brady's compound eyes. "All right, little bee. Any more **brain** waves?"

Brady was pleased to be asked. "Well, actually I do. First of all, Jasper needs time to think. He also needs to have less stimulation. The walls are too cluttered, the lights are too bright, the fan makes noise, and the kids? The kids do **way** too much talking! And then take a look at all those papers he's got! There's no way that Jasper can keep track of all that stuff! And I'm thinking—"

"Oh, I love it when you **think**," Benkin chimed in with a grin.

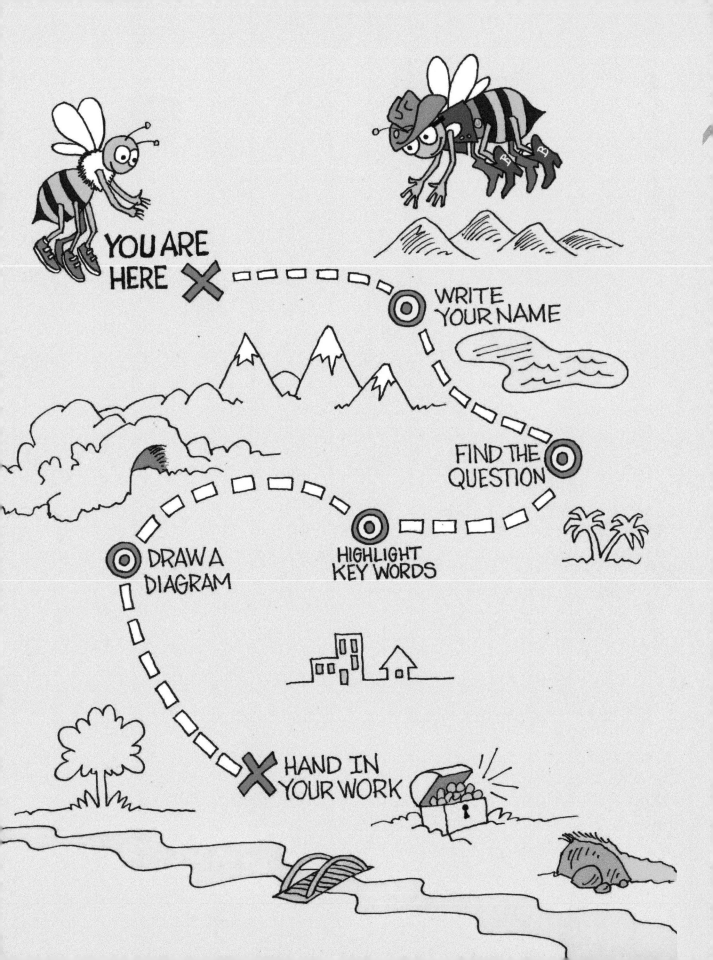

Start

Brady ignored him and continued. "As I was saying, I'm thinking that someone needs to help him start his work. If he just knew how to initiate a task—"

"Whoa, little bee," Benkin interrupted. "'**Initiate** a task'?"

Brady puffed up his hairs. "That means knowing how to start something. If Jasper is feeling overwhelmed with too much work, it might help him to know **how** to start it."

S i m p l e

Benkin nodded his head in agreement, pleasing Brady to no end. "All right, little bee. Let me see if I understand." Benkin started to count off the ideas on all six of his legs.

"First, give him some extra time to think about things." Now it was Brady's turn to nod in approval.

"Second, cut down on the amount of stimulation, like bright lights, loud noises, and walls with too much stuff on them." Brady began flapping his wings with excitement.

Benkin stuck out his third leg and continued. "Don't give him so many papers to organize and sort through. Keep things simple." Brady broke out in a big grin.

"Fourth, teach him **exactly** how to start something, by breaking the task down into small steps." Benkin put up his fifth leg, but wasn't sure what his next point was. He looked to Brady for help.

"Think back to how uncomfortable he was on his seat, and how much his shirt tag bothered him," Brady said, jumping up and down.

"Right," Benkin replied. "It's those little sensory things that no one thinks about that can really throw off his concentration."

"Now look who's using the big words," Brady smirked. "'**Sensory**?'"

"You know what I mean," Benkin replied. "The touchy-feely stuff."

"So what's your sixth point going to be?" Brady prompted Benkin, poking his last leg.

"It's going to be really important for someone to teach Jasper some words to use when he's **feeling** frustrated," Benkin added, lifting his final leg and flying up into the air. "If he could use his words, he might not get so upset."

"Yes!" Brady said, twirling around in circles. He was so pleased with himself, that he didn't notice Queenie until he'd landed right on top of her.

"Ouch!" cried Queenie, waking up from her nap. "I think you've bent one of my wings!"

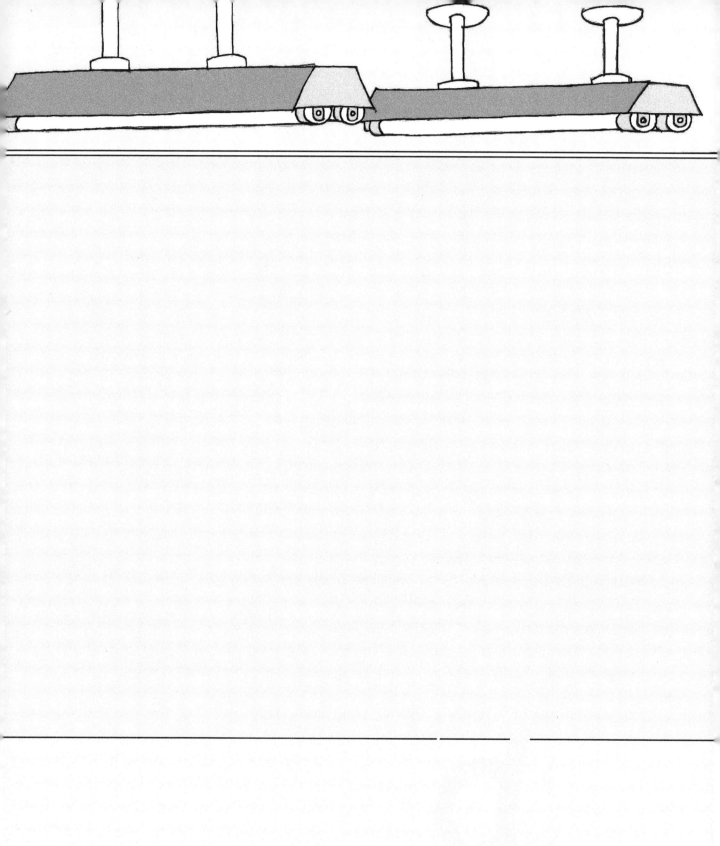

CPSIA information can be obtained
at www.ICGtesting.com
Printed in the USA
BVHW022257220520
579865BV00006B/74